Maya
the Harp
Fairy

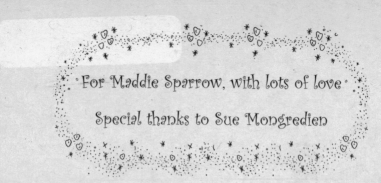

For Maddie Sparrow, with lots of love

Special thanks to Sue Mongredien

ISBN: 978-0-545-10628-3

12 11 10 9 8 7 6 5 4 3   10 11 12 13 14/0

Printed in the U.S.A.

First Scholastic Printing, January 2010

Maya the Harp Fairy

by Daisy Meadows

SCHOLASTIC INC.

New York   Toronto   London   Auckland
Sydney   Mexico City   New Delhi   Hong Kong

The Fairyland Palace

Bana

Wetherbury College

MALL

New Harmony Mall

The Village Hall

The Warehouse

Willow Hill

I'm through with frost, ice, and snow.
To the human world I must go!
I'll form my cool Gobolicious Band.
Magical instruments will lend a hand.

With these instruments, I'll go far.
Frosty Jack, a superstar.
I'll steal music's harmony and its fun.
Watch out, world, I'll be number one!

Contents

Confetti Surprise

"Isn't this a beautiful place for a wedding?" Kirsty Tate said as she and her best friend, Rachel Walker, bounded up the steps of the Wetherbury Hotel. Kirsty was carrying a large present wrapped in sparkly gold paper and tied with a silver bow. Rachel's arms were full of pink flowers. Both girls wore pretty party dresses.

"Oh, *yes!*" Rachel agreed, glancing up at the old manor house, its stone walls covered in rambling ivy. "And the gardens are gorgeous, too," she added.

The hotel was surrounded by emerald-green lawns and large beds of brightly colored flowers. There was a tall stone wall built around the border of the grassy lawn, with elegant archways leading to the rest of the grounds.

"Isn't it wonderful that Kerry decided to have her wedding while you're staying with us for school break, Rachel?" Kirsty remarked as they paused at the top of the steps to wait for Mrs. Tate. "I'm so glad you can come, too!"

Rachel nodded. "It was nice of Kerry to invite us," she replied. "You must have been a *really* good little girl when she was your babysitter, Kirsty!"

Kirsty laughed. "Here's Mom," she said.

Mrs. Tate was hurrying up the steps toward them. "Let's go inside, girls," she said, glancing at her watch. "Kerry's expecting us to be early so we can help finish the decorations for the wedding reception."

The doors to the hotel lobby stood wide open, and Rachel gasped with wonder as they went inside.

"Wow, this is so nice!" she exclaimed. The lobby was painted white and gold, and there were huge vases of sweet-smelling roses everywhere. The carpet was thick, red, and velvety, and a glittering glass chandelier hung from the ceiling. In one corner of the lobby was a man in a tuxedo. He was seated at a baby grand piano, leafing through sheets of music.

"Yes, it's perfect for a wedding, isn't it?" Mrs. Tate agreed. "Girls, will you take the present into the reception room? I'll go and find Kerry. Oh, and Rachel, how about you give me the flowers and take these instead. . . ."

She handed a brown bag full of confetti packets to Rachel. "Will you two scatter some of this confetti on the tables?"

"OK, Mom," Kirsty agreed, as Mrs. Tate rushed off with the flowers.

5

The girls headed down a hallway to the reception room.

"What's that noise?" Rachel asked curiously as they got closer to the open door.

"I don't know," Kirsty replied with a frown. "It sounds like a musical instrument, but it doesn't sound *right*!"

"Oh, I know!" Rachel exclaimed, "It's a harp, but it's very flat. Harp music is usually beautiful and light and airy."

"Well, we *know* why it doesn't sound right," Kirsty whispered. "It's because Maya the Harp Fairy's magic harp is still missing!"

Rachel nodded in agreement. The girls were helping their friends, the Music Fairies, search for their missing magic musical instruments. They made music fun and harmonious in both the human and fairy worlds! The instruments had been stolen by Jack Frost. He had sent his goblins to hide the instruments in and around Wetherbury so they'd be ready for the National Talent Competition that coming weekend. Jack Frost and his goblins had formed a pop group called Frosty and his Gobolicious Band, and they were determined to use the magic of the Music Fairies' special instruments to win first place — a recording contract with MegaBig Records. Rachel and Kirsty were very worried that everyone in the human world would find out about Fairyland if Jack Frost became a famous pop star!

"We still have three magic instruments to find before the talent competition this weekend," Rachel reminded Kirsty as they went into the reception room. "We need to get them *all* back — even if Jack Frost has only *one* of the instruments, its

magic will help his band win!"

"I know," Kirsty agreed, placing the wedding gift on a table with a

few other elegantly wrapped presents.
"We don't have much time left!" She
nudged Rachel. "Look, there's the
harpist."

A woman in a long, silky,
pink dress sat at the
other end of the room.
She had a tall harp of
polished wood in front
of her, and she
plucked at a few
of the strings. As the
girls watched, they
could see that she
was frowning.
The harp was
definitely out
of tune.

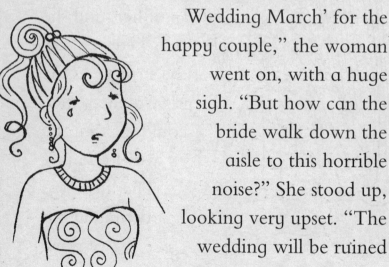

"Oh, hello," the woman called as she
noticed Rachel and Kirsty. "Sorry
about the awful noise." She bit her lip.
"I just can't get my harp in tune. It
sounds terrible! I seem to be all thumbs
today."

"Are you playing at Kerry's wedding?"
Kirsty asked.

"Yes, I'm supposed to be playing 'The
Wedding March' for the
happy couple," the woman
went on, with a huge
sigh. "But how can the
bride walk down the
aisle to this horrible
noise?" She stood up,
looking very upset. "The
wedding will be ruined

if I can't figure out what's wrong!" she cried, rushing from the room in tears.

"Oh, that's awful," Kirsty said, concerned.

"And poor Kerry, too," Rachel added. "It doesn't look like she'll get her harp music after all."

"Well, at least we can make the room look nice for her," Kirsty replied. "Let's decorate the tables!"

Rachel opened the confetti bag. "There are lots of packets of pink and silver sparkly hearts," she said, taking one out. "They'll look pretty, scattered on these snowy white tablecloths."

"And they'll match the pink tulips," added Kirsty, glancing at the crystal vases of flowers that stood on each of the tables.

Rachel put the brown bag down on a nearby table and tried to rip open the confetti. She struggled with the packet and had to use both hands to tug it open in the end.

The packet burst open, and confetti flew out in a shimmering cloud of pink and silver sparkles. The girls were

amazed as the sparkles lingered in the air
and then fizzed around the room in a
flash of dazzling colors.

"Rachel, it's a *fairy!*" Kirsty cried.

Hunt for the Goblin

As the sparkles began to fade, the fairy whizzed over to hover in front of Rachel and Kirsty. She wore a flowing halter dress with a bright swirl pattern.

"Hi, girls!" she cried. "I'm Maya the Harp Fairy."

"Oh, hello, Maya!" Rachel exclaimed

in delight. "Is your harp somewhere close by?"

Maya nodded. "Yes, and the goblins are, too!" she said, twirling down to land lightly on the white tablecloth. "We have to find my harp, or Kerry's wedding will be ruined!"

"Let's start looking for the goblins right away," Kirsty began, but Rachel pointed at the brown bag of confetti packets.

"We'd better do this first or your mom won't be very happy, Kirsty!" she said with a grin.

"My magic can do that in a flash," Maya chimed in. She pointed her wand at the bag and, in a shower of fairy sparkles, all the packets of confetti flew out. They hovered in the air for a second, then burst open with a pop. A

huge cloud of glittering pink and silver
hearts whirled around the room,
scattering themselves on the white
tablecloths.

"Perfect!" Kirsty laughed as the last few
hearts landed neatly in place.

"Now we can go on a goblin hunt!"
Maya said with a smile. "Remember, girls,
Jack Frost has given the goblins a wand
to change the size of the magic musical
instruments. His spell has also made

the goblins little-boy-size, and has taken the green out of their skin. So, they'll be able to blend in with the wedding guests."

"Yes, but the spell didn't work completely, so they still have big noses, ears, and feet!" Kirsty added.

Rachel reached over and pulled a pink tulip from one of the vases. "You can hide in here, Maya," she said.

Maya flew over to the tulip and slipped between the silky pink petals, out of sight. "Let's go, girls!" she whispered. "Where should we look, Rachel?" asked Kirsty as they went into the hallway.

"Let's go back to the lobby and start there," Rachel suggested. She carried Maya's tulip carefully.

As the girls made their way back to the lobby, a man in a tuxedo came hurrying toward them. He looked very annoyed and was mumbling to himself.

"Really, that's no way for one musician to treat another!" he muttered furiously. "I'm going to complain to the hotel manager."

The man was so angry, he barged right past the girls and almost knocked Maya out of the tulip. She grabbed ahold of a petal just in time to stop herself from falling.

"Are you all right, Maya?" asked Kirsty, when the man had disappeared around the corner.

Maya popped her head out of the tulip and nodded.

"I wonder what's the matter with *him*?" said Rachel.

"I think he's the piano player from the lobby," Kirsty replied. "Remember? He was about to start playing when we first got here."

"Listen!" Rachel grabbed her friend's arm. "I hear music!"

Maya and the girls listened. They could all hear ripples of sweet, airy music coming from the lobby just ahead of them.

"That's my harp!" Maya gasped.

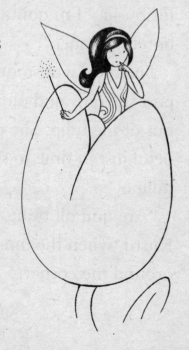

Kirsty and Rachel ran toward the lobby. It was packed with people listening to the beautiful tune. It was so crowded, the girls couldn't see Maya's harp or the harpist.

"What should we do?" Kirsty whispered to Rachel.

"We'll just have to push our way through the crowd as politely as possible!" Rachel whispered back.

The girls began to weave their way through the lobby. Rachel still held Maya's tulip tightly.

"Excuse me," Rachel said to an elderly woman who looked completely entranced by the music. "Could you let us by, please? We want to see who's playing the harp."

"Of course, my dear," the woman replied, moving aside a little. "Isn't it amazing to see such a young boy play so beautifully?"

Rachel and Kirsty exchanged a glance. Now they could see the harpist, plucking at the strings of a beautiful golden harp. He wore a suit with tails and a top hat, but the clothes couldn't disguise his big nose, ears, and feet.

"It's a goblin!" whispered Kirsty.

Musical Statue

The goblin drew his fingers across the strings with a final, rippling flourish, and the audience broke into tremendous applause. Grinning, the goblin stood up and swept his top hat off in a low bow.

"Do you think he's going to play another song?" Rachel asked Kirsty.

"I hope not," Kirsty replied, "because we have no chance of getting Maya's harp back with all these people around!"

The goblin was about to seat himself at the harp again when the crowd suddenly parted to let a tall man through.

He wore a badge that read HOTEL MANAGER. Close behind him was the piano player, who still looked very annoyed.

Kirsty and Rachel watched as the hotel manager walked up to the goblin.

"Thank you very much for your lovely performance," he said with a strained smile. "It was completely unexpected, but everyone enjoyed it. However, it's the piano player's turn to perform now."

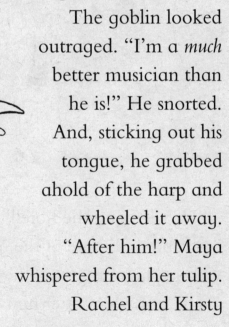

The goblin looked outraged. "I'm a *much* better musician than he is!" He snorted. And, sticking out his tongue, he grabbed ahold of the harp and wheeled it away.

"After him!" Maya whispered from her tulip. Rachel and Kirsty hurried after the goblin, weaving their way in between the people, who were now milling around.

"He's leaving the hotel!" said Kirsty, catching a glimpse of the goblin as he wheeled his harp out of the main entrance. The girls went after him as fast as they could, but it was difficult to keep up while

so many people were around. More
guests were arriving for the wedding, too.
It took a few minutes before Rachel
and Kirsty could leave through the
main doors.

"We lost him!"
Rachel
exclaimed in
dismay.

"No, there
he is!" Kirsty
cried,
pointing
across the
garden.

The goblin was
just escaping through one of the ivy-
covered archways.

Maya fluttered out of the tulip and into

the air as she, Rachel, and Kirsty raced after the goblin. They peeked through the arch and saw him pull an icy wand from inside his jacket. He pointed it at the harp, and the instrument shrank down to pocket-size in the blink of an eye.

"Let's try to grab the harp!" Rachel suggested.

The three friends dashed through the arch, but the goblin heard them coming. He spun around with a shriek of rage.

"Go away, pesky girls!" he roared, snatching the tiny harp from the ground. He slipped it into his pocket and ran off toward another archway.

Rachel, Kirsty, and Maya followed. On the other side of the arch was a beautiful rose garden with marble statues of Greek gods all around. But the goblin was nowhere to be seen.

"He must be here *somewhere*!" Kirsty panted. "There's no other way out!"

Maya and the girls began to search the rose garden. They looked behind every rosebush, but there was no sign of the goblin anywhere.

Suddenly, Rachel clutched Kirsty's arm.

"Look," she said in a low voice. "See that statue under the willow tree at the bottom of the garden?"

Kirsty looked where Rachel was pointing. There was a tall stone wall at the bottom of the rose garden, and next to it was a willow tree. Under the tree stood a marble statue of a woman in a flowing robe. The statue was placed on top of a tall, marble base, and was in shadow, almost hidden by the willow's long, drooping branches.

"The goblin could be hiding under the willow tree!" Rachel went on.

"Let's go and see," Maya said eagerly.

The three friends hurried over to the tree, and Rachel began to part the branches carefully, searching for the goblin.

Meanwhile, Kirsty glanced up at the tall statue. Suddenly, she caught a very quick glimpse of a top hat before it whisked out of sight again.

The goblin's hiding behind the statue!

Kirsty thought. *He must have climbed up onto the base!*

She glanced at Maya and Rachel, then put her finger to her lips and pointed at the statue. They nodded in understanding.

"The base is very high," Kirsty whispered. "Rachel, if you stand on my shoulders, do you think you'd be able to get the harp out of the goblin's pocket?"

"I'll try!" Rachel whispered.

Quietly, the three friends headed over to the statue. But before they could carry out their plan, they heard a shriek of warning high above their heads.

"Look out! There are those horrible girls *and* a dreadful fairy!"

Disappointed, Maya, Rachel, and Kirsty looked up and saw a second goblin sitting on top of the garden wall. He reached down behind the statue and grabbed the goblin with the harp, tugging him up onto the wall.

"Ha, ha!" the goblins jeered, making faces at Maya and the girls. "We win and you lose! You'll never get the magic harp back now!"

And with that, they disappeared over the garden wall.

Cart Chaos

"Oh, no!" Rachel exclaimed. "How are we going to catch them *now*? The wall's too high for us to climb over."

"The wall isn't a problem," Maya replied with a smile, "if you have wings!"

She flew over the girls' heads, showering them with a cloud of multi-colored fairy sparkles from her wand.

Immediately, Rachel and Kirsty became
fairy-size, with glittering wings on their
backs.

"Here we go!" Maya cried, linking
arms with the girls.

Together, all three of them soared up
and over the wall.

"There go the goblins!" Kirsty shouted,
catching a glimpse of them in the distance.

"And it looks like they're heading back toward the hotel!" Rachel added. The goblins were running across the lawn to the hotel entrance.

"I bet there are lots of people inside now, because all the wedding guests will have arrived," said Kirsty, as the goblins dashed into the lobby. "The goblins are probably hoping that they'll be able to hide in the crowd!"

"We need to be careful that they don't spot us," Maya said anxiously.

Rachel, Kirsty, and Maya flew into the lobby. As Kirsty had guessed, it was packed with people! The girls and Maya kept as close as possible to the walls of the room to avoid being seen by the guests.

"There are a lot of fancy wedding hats around!" Rachel gasped, as she zipped up to dodge a large-brimmed, pink straw hat.

"Let's fly higher and see what's happening," Maya said in a low voice, pointing up at the crystal chandelier. They all whizzed upward and perched on one of the sparkling globes of glass.

"There are so many people here," Kirsty remarked, peering down at the wedding guests. "The goblins could be *anywhere*!"

Rachel grinned. "I think I see one!" she said, pointing. "Look at that waiter!"

Kirsty and Maya peered down at a waiter below them. He looked pretty funny — his jacket was too big and came all the way down to his knees! He was pushing a food cart with a beautiful, white, four-tiered wedding cake on it.

"It's the goblin who was on top of the wall!" said Maya. "But where's the goblin with my harp?"

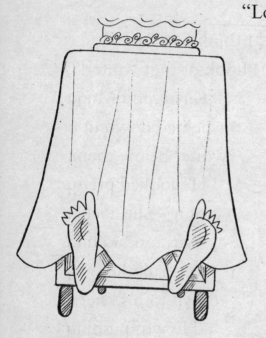

"Look at the bottom shelf of the cart!" Kirsty laughed. The cart was covered with a long white cloth, but Kirsty had spotted two large feet poking out from underneath the material.

"After them!" Maya whispered.

The goblin waiter was wheeling the cart toward the reception room as fast as he could.

"I hope the goblins are careful with Kerry's cake," Kirsty worried as she flew after them. "It would be awful if anything happened to it!"

As the goblin pushed the cart into the reception room, Maya, Rachel, and Kirsty ducked inside, too. They had just enough time to hide behind the sparkly bow on top of one of the wedding presents before the goblin closed the door.

"You can come out now," the waiter said triumphantly to the other goblin.

"We managed to dodge that silly fairy and her human friends!"

The goblin with the harp climbed out from under the tablecloth, grinning happily. But suddenly, the door swung open and a woman in a pretty, rose-colored suit and a white hat hurried in.

"Oh!" Kirsty whispered. "It's Kerry's mother, Mrs. Bolton!"

Mrs. Bolton looked annoyed.

"Oh, you finally brought the cake!" she exclaimed. "We were beginning to wonder where it was."

The goblins looked sheepish. "Well — er —" the goblin waiter began.

"Never mind that now," Mrs. Bolton said impatiently. "Put the cake on that table in the corner, and please hurry!"

The goblins rushed to pick up the cake as Mrs. Bolton stepped out again, closing the door behind her.

"Oh, I can't look!" Kirsty groaned, covering her eyes. The girls and Maya

held their breath as the goblins clumsily lifted the cake off the cart and placed it on the table.

"At least the cake's safe!" Rachel said with a sigh of relief. "Now it's time to get the harp! But how?"

Cake in Crisis

"Any ideas, girls?" asked Maya.

Kirsty and Rachel both thought hard. Below them, the goblins were smirking, looking very pleased with themselves.

"I'm going to play at the wedding!" the goblin with the harp announced proudly. "I'm a *much* better player than that human woman. Her harp sounded horrible!" He pulled Maya's little harp out of his pocket and stroked it lovingly. The second goblin looked on with envy.

Kirsty grinned. "If there's one thing we can always count on, it's the goblins arguing with each other!" she whispered. "Maybe we can get them to argue over the harp?"

"Great idea, Kirsty!" Rachel agreed. "And while they're disagreeing, Maya can swoop down and get it back."

"Go for it, girls!" said Maya.

Rachel and Kirsty flew across to the goblins. Kirsty zoomed toward the goblin who had the harp, while Rachel hurried over to the other one.

"Oh, no!" shrieked the goblin when he saw Kirsty. "Fairies!"

"I just wanted to tell you something," Kirsty said quickly. "I've noticed that other goblin looking at your harp. I'm sure he's going to try to steal it from you!"

The goblin frowned. "I'd like to see him try!" he muttered.

Meanwhile, Rachel was talking to the second goblin.

"Why don't *you* get a turn with the harp?" she said. "I'd like to hear how *you* play."

The goblin looked very sulky.

"*He* won't let me," he grumbled, pointing at the first goblin.

Rachel pretended to look astonished. "Doesn't he ever share?" she asked.

The second goblin shook his head. "No, he's mean!" he replied.

Rachel frowned and said, "I don't think you should let him get away with that!"

"You're right," said the second goblin. "Well, he's going to share *now*!" He dashed across the room and tried to grab the harp from the other goblin.

"Get away!" the first goblin howled, giving him a shove. Soon, the two goblins were rolling around on the floor, wrestling over the harp!

Kirsty and Rachel hovered nearby as Maya fluttered down, looking for an opportunity to grab the harp. But it was tough for her to get close to the fighting goblins.

"Oh, no!" Rachel gasped as the goblins rolled toward the table with the wedding cake on it.

"Maybe this wasn't such a good idea after all!" Kirsty said anxiously.

The goblins bumped into the table leg, and the wedding cake began to wobble dangerously.

"The cake's going to fall!" Kirsty cried.

"Maya, HELP!" Rachel shouted.

Maya glanced up, saw the cake beginning to topple, and instantly waved her wand. A stream of magic sparkles swirled toward the cake and surrounded it, keeping it upright.

Kirsty breathed a sigh of relief. But at that moment, the second goblin managed to knock the tiny harp from the first goblin's hand. Maya, Rachel, and Kirsty watched in dismay as the harp sailed through the air.

"It's heading straight for the wedding cake!" Rachel cried. Before Maya and the girls could do anything, the harp landed right on the top tier of the cake.

"At least the harp is tiny, so it couldn't have damaged the cake very much," Maya reassured the girls. "Now, let's grab the harp before the goblins do!"

The goblins had rushed over to the

table. Both were standing
on their tiptoes, trying to
reach the harp. But as
Maya, Rachel, and
Kirsty flew toward the
cake, the door
suddenly opened
again. Maya grabbed
the girls' hands and
pulled her friends
behind one of the vases
of tulips, just as a girl
wearing a pink silk dress
and a beautiful flower in her hair breezed
into the room.

"That's Kerry's bridesmaid!" Kirsty
whispered. "Isn't her dress beautiful?"

"Oh, please leave that cake alone and
come help me!" the bridesmaid told the

goblins with a smile. "There's still *so* much to do." She glanced at the cake and then gave a gasp of delight. "Oh, Kerry will *love* that harp decoration — it's the perfect finishing touch!" She turned to the goblins. "Follow me," she ordered, grabbing their hands and pulling them over to the door. "You can collect gifts from the guests before the ceremony begins and put them on the table over there."

The goblins glanced anxiously at the harp, but they couldn't take it without the bridesmaid noticing. Maya, Rachel, and Kirsty laughed quietly as the bridesmaid ushered the reluctant goblins out of the room.

"Come along," she said bossily. "The wedding's starting soon, and we've got work to do!"

Here Comes the Bride

As soon as the bridesmaid and goblins had left the room, Maya flew over to the cake and picked up her harp. She drew her fingers gently across the strings, filling the room with magical music.

"The cake *did* look nice with the harp on top," said Kirsty. "It's too bad it won't have one now."

Maya smiled. As her harp transformed back to its Fairyland size, she began to play a special melody. As she did, a glittering spiral of fairy sparkles swirled around the top tier of the cake. Rachel and Kirsty watched in wonder as the top of the cake shimmered and glowed.

"Look, Rachel!" Kirsty cried. "There's a *new* harp on the cake!"

"And it looks exactly like Maya's," Rachel added.

"It looks exactly the same, but there's one big difference." Maya pointed her wand at the harp on the cake. "This one is made of white chocolate, so you can eat it!"

The girls laughed.

"What's that?" Rachel asked suddenly, as she heard the faint sound of sweet music in the distance. "It sounds like *another* harp."

"The wedding's starting!" Kirsty exclaimed.

Quickly, Maya sprinkled the girls with fairy dust. They instantly grew back to their normal size.

"Thank you for everything!" Maya said. "Now I must take my harp back to Fairyland, and *you* must go to Kerry's wedding!"

With a wave, Maya vanished in a mist of glittery sparkles. Following the sound of the harp, Kirsty and Rachel rushed to the large hall where the wedding was being held. They could see the harpist playing at the front of the room.

"Here comes Kerry!" Kirsty whispered as they sat down next to Mr. and Mrs. Tate. "We're just in time!"

Beaming, the girls watched as Kerry, looking beautiful in a long, ivory wedding dress, walked down the aisle to the heavenly sound of the harp.

"The harp sounds amazing, doesn't it?" Rachel sighed happily.

"That's because the magic harp is back in its proper place in Fairyland!" Kirsty replied. "We only have Victoria's violin and Sadie's saxophone to find now!"

THE Music FAIRIES

Maya the Harp Fairy's magic
instrument is safe and sound in
Fairyland! Can Rachel and Kirsty help

Victoria
the Violin Fairy?

Join their next adventure in this special
sneak peek!

Listen to the Band

"I like that song," Rachel Walker said, pointing at the computer screen. She and her best friend, Kirsty Tate, were downloading music from the Internet, using a gift card that Kirsty had received for her birthday.

Kirsty nodded. "Me, too," she said, clicking the mouse to download the song.

Rachel was staying with Kirsty's family for a week over school break — and so far, the girls had been having a very exciting time! A very musical time, too — helping the Music Fairies find their lost magical instruments!

Mr. Tate, Kirsty's dad, came into the room at that moment. "I was just talking to my friend Charles on the phone," he told them. "Kirsty, do you remember him? He works at Wetherbury College and he's been telling me about a really talented band that has been practicing there. He's sure they're going to do well in the National Talent Competition tomorrow."

Kirsty's ears perked up on hearing her dad's words. She and Rachel knew someone else who was determined to go

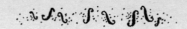

far in the National Talent Competition —
Jack Frost!

"The band is rehearsing at the college,"
Mr. Tate went on, "and Charles asked if
we'd like to go over and listen."

"Oh, yes," Kirsty said. "We'd love to!"

Mr. Tate nodded. "I'll drop you off
there," he replied. "I can't stay myself —
I've got some errands to run."

Rachel smiled and got to her feet. "It'll
be so cool if we get to see the winning
band before the Talent Competition
tomorrow," she said.

"And you never know," Kirsty
murmured as Mr. Tate went to get his
car keys, "we might spot another one of
the magic musical instruments while
we're there. . . ."

RAINBOW magic™

There's Magic in Every Series!

The Rainbow Fairies

The Weather Fairies

The Jewel Fairies

The Pet Fairies

The Fun Day Fairies

The Petal Fairies

The Dance Fairies

Read them all!

■SCHOLASTIC

www.scholastic.com

www.rainbowmagiconline.com

HIT entertainment

RMFAI